Jr Graphic Mysteries™

Bigfoot

A North American Legend

Jack DeMolay

PowerKiDS press™
New York

Published in 2007 by The Rosen Publishing Group, Inc.
29 East 21st Street, New York, NY 10010

First Edition

Editor: Jennifer Way
Book Design: Ginny Chu
Illustrations: Q2A

Library of Congress Cataloging-in-Publication Data

DeMolay, Jack.
Bigfoot : a North American legend / by Jack DeMolay.— 1st ed.
p. cm. — (Jr. graphic mysteries)
Includes index.
ISBN (10) 1-4042-3405-5 — (13) 978-1-4042-3405-5 (library binding) — ISBN (10) 1-4042-2158-1 — (13) 978-1-4042-2158-1 (pbk)
1. Sasquatch—Juvenile literature. I. Title. II. Series.

QL89.2.S2D46 2007
001.944—dc22

2006003390

Manufactured in the United States of America

Contents

BIGFOOT: A NORTH AMERICAN LEGEND

UH, FRED? I DON'T THINK THAT'S A TRESPASSER!
IT WAS A HAIRY, APELIKE CREATURE THAT STOOD NEARLY 8 FEET TALL. IT WOULD BECOME KNOWN AS BIGFOOT.

THE MEN WERE FACED WITH AN ANIMAL THEY HAD NEVER SEEN BEFORE. THEY WERE AFRAID FOR THEIR LIVES.

B-BACK AWAY, FELLAS!

THEY DID THE ONLY THING THEY COULD THINK OF.
SHOOT IT, FRED!

THEY **PROTECTED** THEMSELVES.

DID YOU HIT IT?
I'M NOT SURE. I DON'T THINK SO.

I HAD BETTER CHECK TO SEE IF I HIT HIM.
ARE YOU CRAZY, FRED? THAT THING COULD COME BACK!

YEAH. YOU'RE RIGHT. LET'S GO.

THE CAMP COOK LAUGHED AT THEM. SO DID MOST OF THE OTHER MINERS AND **PROSPECTORS**.

MOST PEOPLE THOUGHT THEY HAD JUST SPENT TOO MUCH TIME IN THE MINES.

TIRED OF BEING MOCKED, THE THREE MEN RETURNED TO THEIR CABIN.

THEY MIGHT HAVE BEEN **CONVINCED** IT WAS ALL A BAD DREAM.
SO, HAVING A HARD TIME BELIEVING WHAT HAPPENED THEMSELVES, THEY WENT TO BED.

BUT THEY DIDN'T SLEEP FOR LONG.
SNAP
CRACK
WHAT WAS THAT?

DO YOU THINK IT'S THE GUYS MESSING WITH US?
I-I DON'T KNOW.

WHAT IF IT'S THAT BEAST TRYING TO GET US?

WHAT SHOULD WE DO?
WE SHOULD GET OUT OF HERE!

I DON'T THINK GOING OUTSIDE IS SUCH A GREAT IDEA, FELLAS.

FINALLY THE NOISES STOPPED.
IS IT OVER?

IT'S GONE. I HOPE.

THEY WAITED FOR MORNING AND PACKED THEIR BAGS TO LEAVE.
I DON'T SEE ANYTHING.
IF THE MEN HAD CHECKED THE GROUNDS, THEY MIGHT HAVE SEEN THE TRAMPLED BUSHES AROUND THEIR CABIN.

THE MEN ALSO FAILED TO SEE CLAW MARKS ON THE OUTSIDE WALLS OF THE CABIN.
DO YOU THINK IT'S WAITING FOR US?

THEY DID NOT SEE THE TRACKS THE BEAST HAD LEFT BEHIND, EITHER.
I DOUBT IT.

THEY DIDN'T LOOK.
WE SHOULD KEEP MOVING.
THE THREE MEN RAN FAR AWAY. THEY WERE AFRAID THE MONSTER MIGHT COME BACK FOR THEM.

FRED AND HIS FRIENDS WERE TALKED ABOUT AFTER THEY LEFT.

EVERYONE LAUGHED AT THEIR STORY, ESPECIALLY THE NEW PROSPECTOR.

BUT HE WOULDN'T LAUGH FOR LONG.

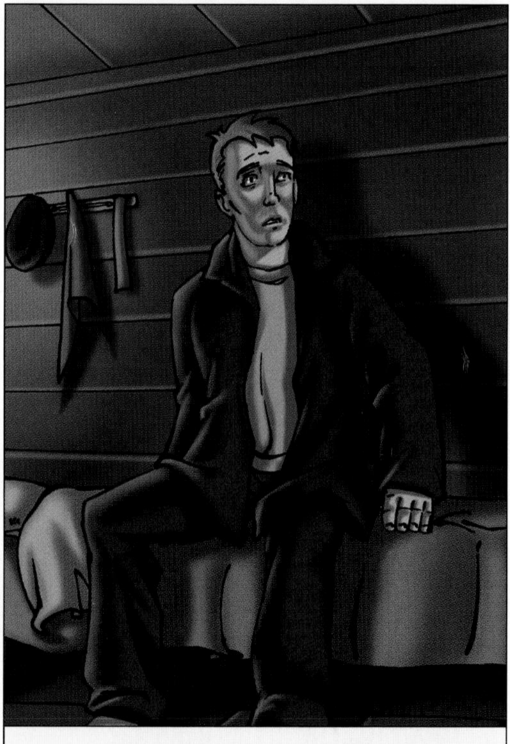

ONE NIGHT WHILE HE WAS SLEEPING, HE WAS AWOKEN BY NOISES OUTSIDE HIS CABIN.

IN THE MORNING THE PROSPECTOR FOUND THE THINGS THAT FRED AND HIS MEN HAD MISSED.

HE FOUND SCRATCHES ON HIS CABIN WALLS.

HE FOUND BRUSH AND SMALL TREES PUSHED OVER.

IN THE MUDDY TRAIL LEADING TO HIS CABIN, HE FOUND FOOTPRINTS!

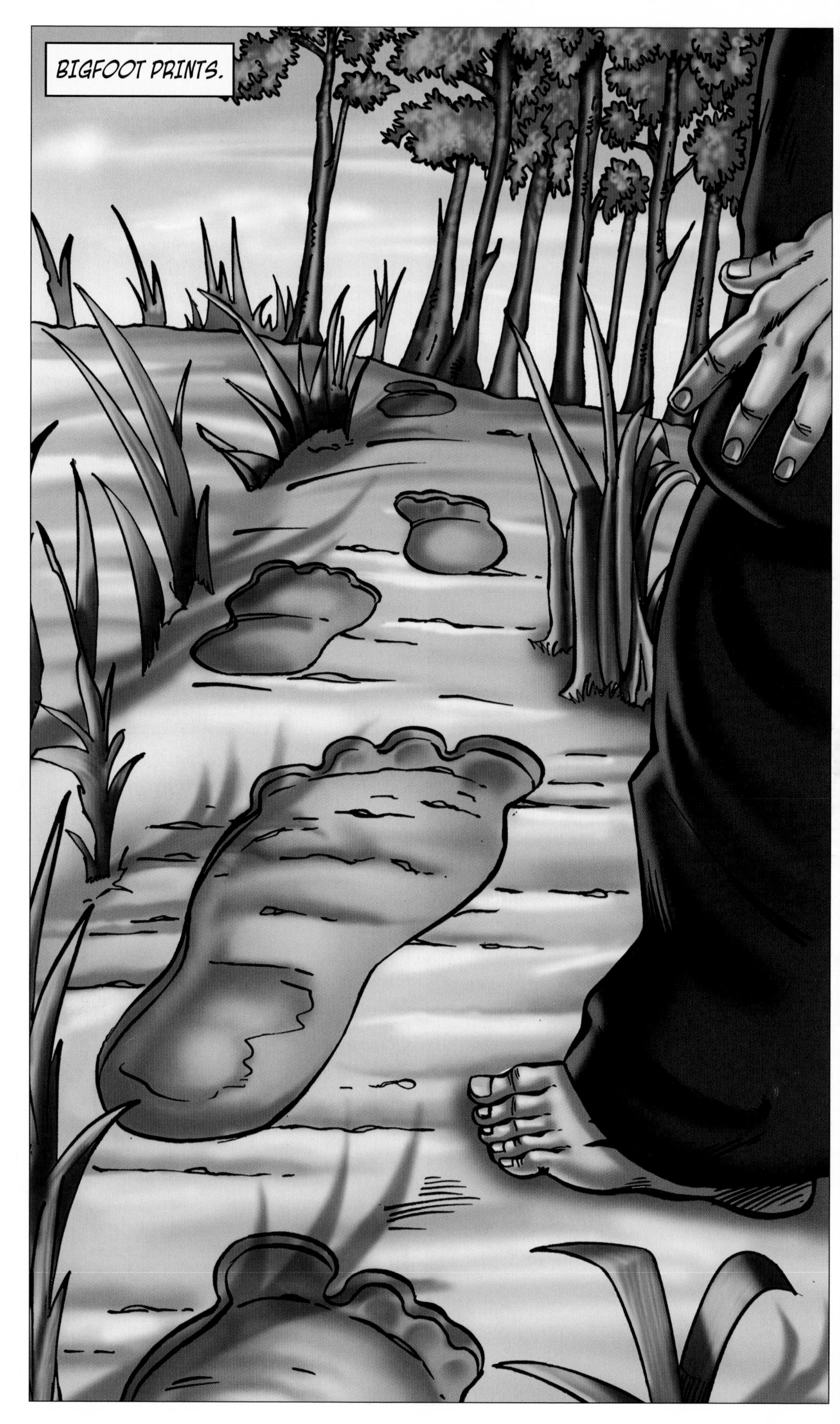
BIGFOOT PRINTS.

IN THE YEARS THAT FOLLOWED, THE **LEGEND** OF BIGFOOT GREW.

IN 1967, THE FIRST **PHOTOGRAPHIC EVIDENCE** OF BIGFOOT APPEARED.

ROGER PATTERSON AND BOB GIMLIN SHOT A HOME MOVIE OF BIGFOOT AT PINE BLUFF CREEK, CALIFORNIA.

THE HOME MOVIE WAS SHOWN ON TELEVISION ACROSS THE UNITED STATES. IT MADE BIGFOOT FAMOUS.
MARTHA! KIDS! GET IN HERE QUICK!
YOU'VE GOT TO SEE THIS!

SINCE THEN OTHER PEOPLE HAVE HUNTED FOR BIGFOOT.

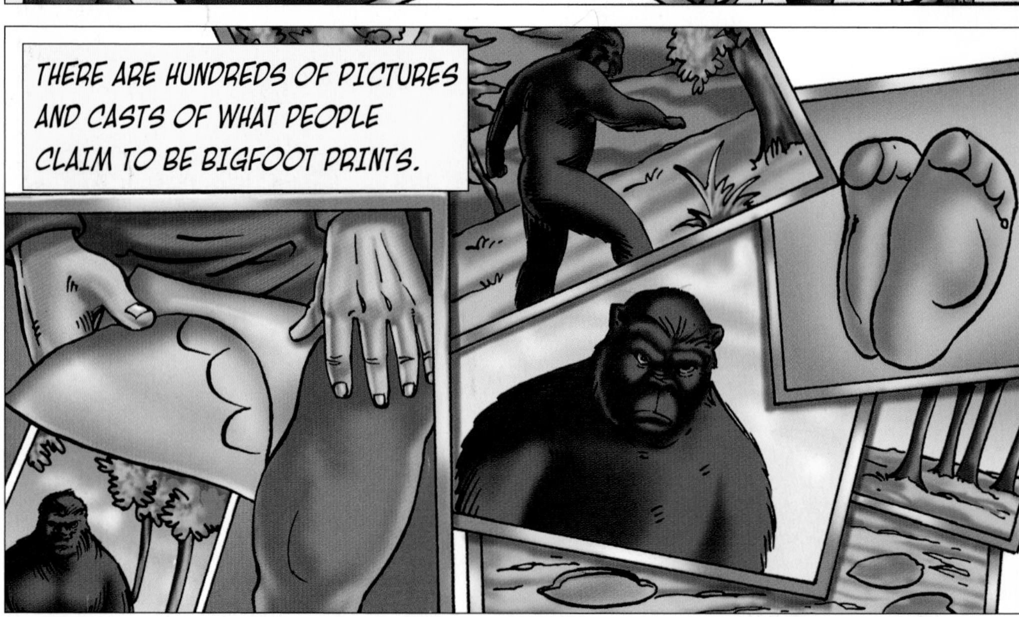
THERE ARE HUNDREDS OF PICTURES AND CASTS OF WHAT PEOPLE CLAIM TO BE BIGFOOT PRINTS.

TO THIS DAY THERE HAS BEEN NO REAL EVIDENCE OF BIGFOOT.
NO BIGFOOT BONES. NO BIGFOOT **FOSSILS.** NO BIGFOOT HAIR.

MOST SCIENTISTS THINK THE EVIDENCE PROVIDED WAS THE WORK OF **PRANKSTERS.**
WITHOUT SOLID EVIDENCE I DOUBT THE EXISTENCE OF BIGFOOT.

CAN YOU SAY FOR SURE THAT BIGFOOT DOESN'T EXIST?
NO. NO, I CANNOT.

SOME PEOPLE THINK THESE PHOTOS AND FOOTPRINTS ARE **HOAXES**. OTHERS BELIEVE IT IS EVIDENCE THAT BIGFOOT EXISTS.

FOR NOW WE CAN ONLY GUESS ABOUT WHETHER BIGFOOT EXISTS.

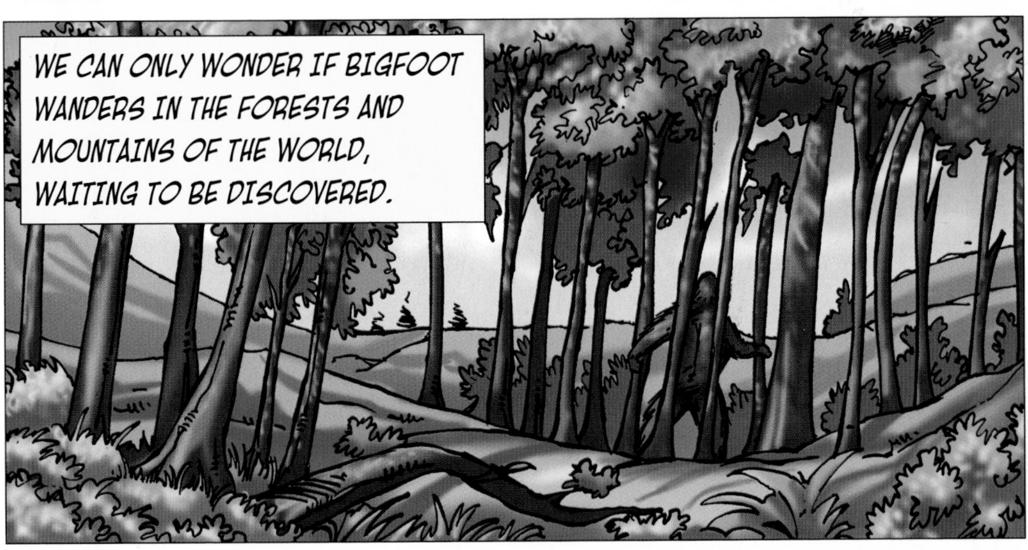
WE CAN ONLY WONDER IF BIGFOOT WANDERS IN THE FORESTS AND MOUNTAINS OF THE WORLD, WAITING TO BE DISCOVERED.

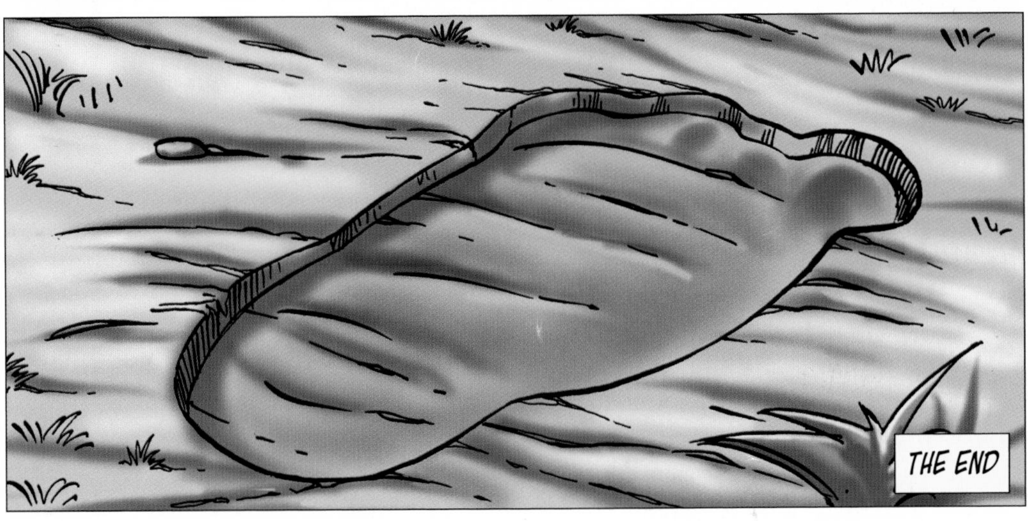
THE END

Did You Know?

- Like the United States, both Canada and Asia have their own story of Bigfoot. In Canada it is known as Sasquatch, which means "hairy giant," and in Asia it is called the yeti.
- Willow Creek, California, calls itself the capital of Bigfoot country. There is a wooden life-size statue of a Bigfoot in the center of town.
- Some scientists believe that Bigfoot is actually a large ape thought to have died out long ago called *Gigantopithecus blacki*.
- In 1972, a man named Allen Berry claimed to have recorded the voice of Bigfoot in the High Sierra Mountains of California.
- Bigfoot first received that name in 1958 when a bulldozer operator named Jerry Crew found huge footprints in Humboldt County, California.
- In Skamania County, Washington, it is against the law to kill a Bigfoot. People can be fined $10,000 or sent to jail.

Glossary

convinced (kun-VINST) To have made a person believe something.

evidence (EH-vuh-dunts) Facts that prove something.

fossils (FAH-sulz) The hardened remains of dead animals or plants.

hoaxes (HOHKS-ez) Things that have been faked.

legend (LEH-jend) A story, passed down through the years, that cannot be proved.

photographic (foh-tuh-GRA-fik) Having to do with pictures that have been taken by a camera.

pranksters (PRANK-sturz) People who play tricks on others.

prospectors (PRAH-spek-terz) People who search an area for gold.

protected (pruh-TEKT-ed) Kept from harm.

trampled (TRAM-puld) Squashed down.

trespassers (TRES-pas-urz) People who enter an area without permission.

uninhabited (un-in-HA-but-ed) Having to do with an area in which no people live.

Index

Web Sites

Due to the changing nature of Internet links, the Rosen Publishing Group, Inc., has developed an online list of Web sites related to the subject of this book. This site is updated regularly. Please use this link to access the list:
www.powerkidslinks.com/jgm/bigfoot/